GWYNETH REES

SUPER CATS

Illustrated by
BECKA
MOOR

BLOOMSBURY
CHILDREN'S BOOKS

LONDON OXFORD NEW YORK NEW DELHI SYDNEY

BLOOMSBURY CHILDREN'S BOOKS
Bloomsbury Publishing Plc
50 Bedford Square, London WC1B 3DP, UK

BLOOMSBURY, BLOOMSBURY CHILDREN'S BOOKS and the
Diana logo are trademarks of Bloomsbury Publishing Plc

First published in Great Britain in 2019 by Bloomsbury Publishing Plc

A catalogue record for this book is available from the British Library

ISBN: PB: 978-1-4088-9419-4; eBook: 978-1-4088-9420-0

2 4 6 8 10 9 7 5 3

Typeset by RefineCatch Limited, Bungay, Suffolk
Printed and bound in Great Britain by CPI Group (UK) Ltd, Croydon CR0 4YY

To find out more about our authors and books visit www.bloomsbury.com
and sign up for our newsletters

In memory of my dad, Cameron,
who loved cats

25th April 1926–28th December 2018

CHAPTER ONE

A PURR-FECTLY ORDINARY FAMILY OF FELINES

Tagg was born in the spring – the first of five tabby kittens born to his mother, Melody, and father, Chester. It was Melody's second litter and this time she had her kittens in the family wardrobe, on top of her human's cleanest and most comfortable sweater.

Melody and Chester were fairly laid back when it came to kitten-rearing. Melody prided

herself on being able to lick a kitten spotless in two minutes flat, and Chester didn't bat an eyelid if one of his offspring tried to climb a tree or went to investigate next-door's cat flap without asking. All kittens got into trouble, he said – especially the adventurous ones. They either learned from their mistakes, or they lost their nine lives rather quickly.

'I know that sounds harsh,' Melody told the kittens, 'but your father is right.

The sooner you realise how perilous the outside world can be, the sooner you will learn not to do stupid or dangerous things.'

Tagg, who was a handsome tabby kitten with a white tummy, white paws and a thick stripy tail, glanced shyly at his father. All the kittens were in awe of Chester – a huge stocky ginger cat with dark green eyes. 'Did you do any stupid or dangerous things when you were young, Dad?' he asked curiously.

'I don't believe I did many *stupid* things,' Chester replied. '*Dangerous* perhaps – at least for an ordinary cat.'

'What sort of dangerous things?' Tagg was so excited to hear more that he forgot to ask what his father meant by 'ordinary'.

'Nothing you need to know about at the moment,' Melody told him swiftly.

As the months passed, Tagg noticed that his parents were treating him differently to the other kittens. He wouldn't say he was their *favourite* exactly, but he was certainly the one they scolded and fussed over the most, and he was always the one Chester took hunting.

It wasn't long before Tagg knew far more than his siblings about the arts of catching mice, stalking birds and correctly judging whether your prey would fit through the cat flap *before* you made a complete fool of yourself with a dead squirrel.

As Tagg approached six months of age, he was the only kitten of his litter still living with his parents, and it wasn't because no humans had wanted him. Twice Tagg had been rehomed to a new human household, and twice his parents had come that same night to retrieve him. Each time his father had carried him home by the scruff of his neck, until in the end their humans had given up and let him stay.

Tagg didn't really mind. He liked their comfortable home in its quiet, tree-lined street. He had a cat flap to come and go as he pleased, a plentiful supply of food and water and a well-stocked fish pond in the garden (even if it was covered with an irritating metal mesh).

On his six-month birthday, Tagg was excited as he scampered out into the garden.

'Uncle Bill has caught a mouse for me to play with,' he called out to his parents, who were curled up together on the grass. Wild Bill, who was Tagg's great-uncle, lived on his own in the rickety summer house at the bottom of their garden.

'Wait, Tagg,' Chester said urgently. 'We need to talk to you.'

'Yes, Dad.' Tagg sat down obediently, hoping this wouldn't take too long. His great-uncle wasn't as sprightly as he used to be and Tagg was worried the elderly cat might not be able to stop his gift from scampering away if he didn't get there quickly. That was if Wild Bill could manage to refrain from eating it. After all, it was no secret that he was extremely partial to a bit of fresh mouse.

'Now that you are six months old, we want to tell you something about our family,' Melody began. 'It's a secret you must never repeat to anyone. Do you understand?'

Tagg's ears pricked up immediately. He loved secrets. 'Of course, Mum.'

'Good.' She looked at Chester to continue.

'Although your mother and I may seem like ordinary cats,' Chester began, 'we both have a very special ability. A *super* ability, if you like.'

'Wow!' Tagg was even more excited. 'Do you mean you have super*powers*?' His mother had often told him bedtime stories about cats with superpowers, but he had always assumed the adventures were made up.

'That is exactly what I mean,' Chester replied.

'Wow!' Tagg exclaimed again. 'So what can you do?' Maybe his mother and father could fly! Or turn invisible! That would explain how they were so good at creeping up on him whenever he was scratching at the carpet or stealing food from the kitchen table.

'Well ...' Chester sounded like he was making the most serious of announcements as he stated, 'your mother has extremely sharp claws.'

Tagg let out a spluttery mew of mirth. He couldn't help it.

Chester hissed. 'This is not a laughing matter!'

'Sorry.' Tagg struggled to get his face straight again as he stammered, 'It's just … well … surely … don't *all* cats have those?'

'Allow me to demonstrate,' Melody said with a twinkle in her eye as she lifted one of her paws and stretched out the digits. Her claws seemed to go blurry for a few moments, then, all of a sudden, they changed into curved blades that radiated an odd, gleaming energy. The miniature swords looked totally unreal on the ends of her dainty white paws.

'Yikes!' Tagg blurted out. 'I mean, that's … *awesome*!'

Melody turned around to face her kitten.

'My super claws will cut through anything, Tagg,' she said. 'And I mean *anything*.'

Tagg gulped. Looking nervously at his father, he asked, 'So what can you do, Dad?'

Chester crouched down on his back legs and began to swing his hindquarters like any cat preparing to spring. But then he leaped off the ground and up, up, up, as high as the roof of the house and right over it.

Tagg raced around to the front of the house as fast as he could, but by the time he got there his father had vanished. 'Where is he?' Tagg mewed in wonder as he searched the sky.

'Oh … several streets away by now, I expect,' Melody replied as she joined him. 'His back legs are *extremely* powerful.' She gave Tagg's head a gentle lick. 'I know it's a lot to take in, but don't worry. You'll be used to the idea by the time your own power develops.'

'M-my own p-power ... ?' Tagg gasped.

'That's right. You might have super claws or super strength, or you may develop something completely different. Whatever your power is, your father and I will be here to teach you how to use it properly. That is why we couldn't let you leave us like your brothers and sisters.'

Tagg suddenly thought of something. 'But how come *I'm* the only one? What makes *me* so special?'

'Nobody knows why only one kitten in each litter is born with superpowers,' Melody explained. 'But I *knew* you were the one from the moment you were born.

It was exactly how I felt when your brother Rowdy was born. He was the super kitten from our first litter.'

'Rowdy?' It was the first time Tagg had heard the name. 'What superpower does he have? Where is he now?'

'He decided that he wanted to go off on his own and explore other places. He has super strength, like Chester.' Her voice was light but Tagg thought she looked sad. 'Now, didn't you say something about a mouse?'

'Oh yes … wait … does Uncle Bill know about this?'

'Of course. He's a super cat too – at least he *was*.'

'Really?' Tagg immediately thought of the impressive stench of cat wee in the summer house. His mother had told him that it was just as well Uncle Bill's wee was so powerful because it meant any strange cats steered well clear. Tagg asked uncertainly, 'So does he have super *wee*?'

Melody let out a little snort. 'Of course not. His wee is quite ordinary, believe it or not. There's nothing unusual about a male cat spraying his territory, though your uncle does take it a bit far. No ... Wild Bill had super *teeth*. They could bite through anything – glass, wood, metal, vets' instruments ... And if he clamped on to something – or some-body – there wasn't anything you could do to shake him loose!'

'Wow! That sounds *mega* awesome.'

'It was. Unfortunately, all his teeth have fallen out now and he has no superpower left. And speaking of Uncle Bill ...'

'I'd better go!' Tagg gasped, suddenly thinking of his promised mouse.

'Make sure you eat it all up afterwards, Tagg,' his mother reminded him. 'You know how I feel about cats who only *play* with their food.'

Tagg found his great-uncle sitting outside the summer-house door, thoroughly washing his whiskers.

'Oh no,' Tagg miaowed crossly. 'You've eaten it already, haven't you?'

The older cat looked up and gave him a calm blink. 'I most certainly have, young fella. Fresh mouse can be extremely hard to resist if you're that way inclined. That's why I told you to come straight away. Now off you go while I take my nap.' Wild Bill napped after every meal these days, saying that at his age he couldn't be expected to digest food *and* stay awake at the same time.

Looking at his great-uncle now, Tagg found it hard to believe that the elderly tabby cat with absent teeth and patchy fur had once been a super cat.

He couldn't keep the excitement from his voice as he blurted, 'Mum and Dad just told me about their superpowers!'

'Time you knew,' the older cat grunted matter-of-factly. 'So how does it feel to be the son of Feline Force One?'

'Feline Force One?' Tagg asked.

'That was their secret-agent code name. Of course, there were others – Feline Force Two, Feline Force Three, Feline Force Four and such like. Me – I always worked alone.

My code name was The Gnasher.' He gave a purr of pride.

'Wait – you were *secret agents*?' Tagg wondered what other information his parents had left out.

'That's right. Our boss, the top cat, was called Topaz. She lived at H H with the leader of the humans.'

'H H?' Tagg asked.

'Human Headquarters. It's in the middle of the biggest human city. Anyway, the top human at the time was a real cat lover and he often talked to Topaz about his worries. She learned about all the problems in this country, and that's how we got our missions. When a different human leader came into power, Topaz was prepared to stay and help her too, only this one was allergic to cats and she found herself banished.'

'That's terrible!'

'It certainly was. Topaz was forced to close down the whole operation. After that we moved here. Your parents had kittens and I lost my last few teeth.' He belched and Tagg caught a strong whiff of freshly devoured mouse.

'Mum told me about Rowdy,' Tagg said.

Wild Bill grunted. 'Too headstrong for his

own good, that one. Took off without a mew to anyone. Haven't heard from him for almost two summers now – goodness knows where he went.' Wild Bill yawned. 'Now … if you don't mind, I've some serious sleeping to do.' And two minutes later Wild Bill was gently snoring.

CHAPTER TWO

THE SURPRISE VISITOR

A few days later, Tagg was inside the summer house listening to his great-uncle's stories about the crime-fighting days of his youth. As Tagg rested his chin on his paw, eager to hear more, they were interrupted by Melody calling to them from outside. She sounded cross.

'What's wrong?' Wild Bill asked, as he and Tagg joined her.

'It's the big hairy human. He won't budge from my favourite spot on the sofa.'

'Could be dead?' Wild Bill suggested. 'When they're dead they stop moving.'

'Of course he's not *dead*,' Melody snapped impatiently. 'He's watching some other humans chasing a ball on the TV.'

'I knew an indoor cat whose human died on the sofa and my pal didn't get fed for *three days*,' Wild Bill continued as if she hadn't spoken. 'When his water bowl dried up my friend was forced to drink water from the toilet like a dog!'

As his mother and uncle discussed how to make humans vacate sofas, Tagg started to chase a buzzy fly. When he eventually caught and ate it, he remembered his mother warning him that flies were dirty little insects that carried germs around on their feet. Flies could be swatted but not eaten. Spiders, on the other hand, were much cleaner, although not as tasty, and you had to watch you didn't knock into a web and get sticky stuff all over your nose.

He glanced at his mother, hoping she hadn't noticed, and was relieved she was still deep in conversation with Uncle Bill.

Tagg had a sudden exciting idea. What if his superpower was flying? Imagine being able to soar up into the sky like a bird! Imagine being able to swoop around *chasing* birds! How cool would that be? He could even rescue other kittens from treetops when they got stuck!

Just as he was imagining what colour cape he might wear – superheroes always wore capes on the humans' big TV screens – he heard a noise above him.

As Tagg looked upwards, a roof tile came hurtling down towards them, CRASHING on to the stone patio!

Tagg half expected to see his father on the roof – Chester sometimes misjudged his own strength in relation to everyday objects and situations. But instead he saw the most beautiful cat balanced carefully on their roof. She was slim with sleek silver-grey fur and a shimmery tail, which was currently swishing from side to side.

'Glamour, what are *you* doing here?' Melody called up to her in surprise.

'Hello, Melody ... Wild Bill ... And is this a new kitten I see?' the strange female sang out in a tuneful miaow as she jumped down from the conservatory roof to the garden wall, before landing elegantly on the ground.

'Never mind hello ... you could've knocked one of us out with that tile. Can't afford to lose any more brain cells at my age, you know!' grumbled Uncle Bill.

'It's so good to see you!' Melody exclaimed as the two cats sniffed each other in greeting. Seeing Tagg staring, she told him, 'Glamour is a super cat like us, Tagg. So is her mate,

Flash. We used to work together.' She turned back to the other cat. 'So how are you? Are you still living above the fish and chip shop in Stoke Mewington?'

Tagg spotted movement on the patio and saw Chester returning from his morning prowl.

'So where is Flash?' Melody was asking.

Glamour's purr faded as she cried out in a distressed mew, 'I don't know! That's why I'm here, Melody! I need your help! He's gone missing.'

'*Missing?* When? How?'

Glamour quickly explained how her mate had come here from Stoke Mewington two days ago to get hold of some tickets for a big concert. 'He said he would be back in twenty minutes, but I still haven't heard from him.'

Tagg couldn't help butting in. 'No way! Stoke Mewington is a whole day's journey away from here.'

'Not when you have super speed, like Flash,' said Chester, coming up behind them.

'What concert?' Melody asked.

'It's happening at midday today inside some abandoned factory building. Flash was getting the tickets as a surprise for our kitten. Her favourite band is playing – One Purr.'

'One Purr! They're awesome!' Tagg blurted, feeling prickles of excitement in his spine as his tail bushed up slightly. One Purr was the coolest, most successful cat pop band in the country. They were absolutely amazing and totally *famous*!

Far too famous to be playing in some old factory in Tagg's home town!

'Never heard of 'em,' Wild Bill scoffed, sounding bored.

'Yes, you have,' Melody said impatiently. 'The drummer's a super cat. Thumper, he's called. Shoots firebolts from his tail. He accidently burned down their last venue. There was a big hoo-ha about it. It even made the human news!'

'It must be in the old factory on the edge of town,' Chester said. 'That's the only one that the humans don't use any more. But who's organised a concert there? And why haven't we heard about it until now?'

'Apparently, the building has just been sold to some eccentric human scientist, and the scientist's cat is organising this

concert. But listen, there's something else … three other super cats have gone missing from Stoke Mewington recently.'

Melody's eyes were wide. 'Which other super cats?'

'The elastic couple – Bendy and Slinky.'

You mean Feline Force Five,' Wild Bill muttered under his breath.

'And a Siamese I've never met, called Nemesissy. Her power is hypnotising humans. All three of them disappeared in the past two weeks and nobody has heard from them.'

There was a pause as the adult cats all looked very serious and thoughtful.

'We should contact Topaz and the other super cats in the organisation,' Chester finally said. 'I know where to find Feline Force Four, so I'll start with them.'

'OK, and Glamour and I will go to this concert and see if Flash is there,' Melody said.

'I'll come with you!' Tagg said, bouncing up and down with excitement.

'No, Tagg, I'll be too busy to keep an eye on you,' Melody said. 'I might lose you in the crowd.'

'But I really want to see One Purr!' Tagg protested.

'Do as you're told, Tagg,' Chester ordered him sternly. 'It will be safer if you stay at home. I don't want you leaving until I get back. I should only be away for a day or two.'

'Be careful, Chester,' Melody said, rubbing his nose with her own.

Tagg watched as his father confidently padded across the lawn, his powerful tail held upright.

'My kitten is here too,' Glamour told them. 'Can she stay with Tagg while we check out the concert?'

'Of course. Tagg will keep her company, won't you?'

As Tagg grunted in reply, Wild Bill said, 'You can both join me for my morning nap, if you like. You youngsters nowadays don't sleep nearly enough.'

'Mum, *please*!' Tagg tried again desperately, while Glamour trotted off. 'You *have* to let me come with you!'

'Absolutely NOT!' his mother hissed, showing him all her teeth this time. 'You don't have your superpower yet and this could be dangerous. You'll stay here and be nice to Glamour's kitten.'

Tagg cringed, knowing better than to keep

arguing. He couldn't believe his mother could be this cruel. One Purr was playing! If only his superpower would hurry up and arrive!

As Melody followed Glamour around to the front of the house, Tagg put his head down, made his ears flat and sulkily followed Wild Bill towards the summer house.

Another boring afternoon in the garden awaited ... Unless ...

Tagg checked behind him, just in case his mother or father should reappear. The coast was clear. Wild Bill had gone inside the summer house.

Tagg took a deep breath and thought about One Purr. This was his chance! And he had to take it now, before Glamour's kitten arrived!

Before he had time to change his mind, he bolted through the hole in the fence that led to the neighbouring garden.

CHAPTER THREE

SUGARFOOT AND THE CAT CONCERT

Tagg reached the street just in time to see his mother and Glamour cross the road and dodge underneath a parked van. Checking that the road was clear of traffic, he raced after them.

At first the two grown-up cats were moving so fast Tagg feared he would lose them. As they left their familiar neighbourhood behind, he could feel his heart thumping rapidly in

his chest as he struggled to keep up without giving himself away. If only he had super speed! Or better still, super speed *and* the power to be invisible! Did super cats ever have more than one superpower? he wondered. What if you could inherit one power from each of your parents? That would be *really* cool!

Eventually, Melody and Glamour stopped in front of a high metal fence. It was too tall to climb or jump over and it had scary-looking signs at various points, bearing human writing and pictures of nasty dogs against a yellow background.

Tagg crouched down out of view as Melody unleashed her super claws and began to carve out a cat-sized hole in the fence. Glamour stood back as sparks of red-hot metal flew out.

Tagg was so busy watching his mother that he didn't hear the light feline footsteps creeping up behind him. Only when he felt the tickle of whiskers at his tail did he realise he was not alone.

'You know she really ought to be wearing protective goggles when she does that,' hissed a high-pitched voice.

Tagg whirled round to see a jet-black female kitten with dancing green eyes grinning at him. The kitten didn't seem the least bit bothered by his mother's super claws.

'Oh look ...' She lifted a pure-white front paw to point, and Tagg couldn't help staring at it since it looked so out of place on her otherwise completely black body. 'They're in!'

Tagg saw that she was right. Melody and Glamour had jumped through the hole and were setting off across the wasteland to the factory. He turned back to the strange kitten. 'Who *are* you? And what are you doing here?'

'Same thing as you, I expect,' she answered cheekily. 'Trying to get into this concert. Thanks to laser-claws there, that shouldn't be a problem now!'

Tagg felt his tail bush up. 'What do you know about super cats?'

'Plenty.' She laughed. 'My mum and dad are super cats.'

It suddenly dawned on Tagg who this kitten was. 'Wait ... is your mum Glamour? Have you been following me?'

'Of course! I wasn't going to be left behind. I'm Sugarfoot, by the way.' She lifted up her single white paw.

Tagg slowly raised his own. 'Tagg,' he grunted as they high-fived.

'Come on,' Sugarfoot miaowed confidently. 'I don't want to miss the start of the concert.'

As they scampered across the huge expanse of wasteland towards the factory, Tagg asked, 'When did you find out your parents were super cats?'

'I've always known,' purred Sugarfoot. 'Isn't it cool, how they all worked together as secret agents, getting to hunt down super villains and stuff?'

'Yeah, it must have been … cool,' Tagg agreed, trying not to sound nervous. Super villains had often appeared in his mother's bedtime stories, but he'd only just realised that if super cats were real then it was possible the scary villains were too!

'Mum told me she thinks a super villain might be targeting super cats,' Sugarfoot said. 'She's worried that's what's happened to my dad.' She looked frustrated as she added, 'He wouldn't just not come home. I wish my mum would let me help, but she's says it's too dangerous until my superpower comes in.'

Tagg was just about to admit he didn't have his own power yet either, when they started to hear noises coming from the abandoned building up ahead. 'I wonder how they got One Purr to come here,' Tagg mewed thoughtfully. One Purr travelled all around the country on tour and they usually played in much posher venues. Tickets to see them were rumoured to cost as much as twenty tins of sardines each.

'I don't know.' Sugarfoot shrugged. 'But there's only one way to find out. Come on. Let's go inside.'

Luckily, there were several missing panes of glass in the windows, which made it easy to climb in, and it wasn't long before Tagg and Sugarfoot were standing at the back of a massive crowd. Tagg felt giddy as he looked around. There must be hundreds of cats here, of all shapes, sizes and colours.

It seemed they had arrived just in time. At one end of the makeshift concert hall a large brown Burmese male cat was standing in front of a microphone addressing everyone.

'In a short while, our generous host will be coming onstage to say a few words. But before that ...' he gave a dramatic pause, '... our band is here and ready to start the concert! Queen cats and tomcats, teen cats and kittens, please put your paws together and let's hear your best catcalls for the most successful cat band in the country ... the one and only ... ONE PURR!'

Excited catcalls filled the hall and Sugarfoot looked ready to swoon as four of the coolest boy cats in the land leaped on to the stage wearing dark glasses and diamond-studded collars. As the lead singer performed his trademark wiggle, all the young females in the audience let out high-pitched yowls and ear-shattering catcalls.

'It's THEM! It's really THEM!' Sugarfoot

shouted, and she started to dance as soon as the band began to play.

One Purr had become famous after winning a talent contest, and it was easy to see why they were so popular. Tagg stared in awe at the long-haired ginger drummer. His drum kit consisted of polished white animal skulls of varying sizes and the sticks he was using looked like dog thigh bones. The lead singer's voice was pitch-perfect, and the guitarist's claws plucked at the strings so fast that Tagg wondered if they were normal claws or super ones. It was also the first time he'd seen a fish-scale xylophone. He'd heard they were tricky instruments to play but this cat made it look easy. Soon Tagg was yowling out the band's songs and bopping his tail end in time to the beat.

Suddenly, Sugarfoot was hissing in his ear and he saw her tail was slightly bushed up. 'Come with me! Quick!'

Tagg followed her to the side of the hall in alarm. 'What is it?'

'I just saw our mums. We need to keep out of their way.'

Tagg looked to where she was pointing and saw Melody and Glamour in conversation with some other cats.

After the final song, the audience cat-called and caterwauled their appreciation as One Purr bowed and waved before retreating backstage.

When the big brown Burmese reappeared, nobody could hear him, even though his microphone was turned up as high as it would go. Finally, the noise died down enough for

him to address the crowd. He thanked One Purr and announced that everyone would be given a signed sardine by the band before they left.

'Now, please welcome your host for this evening and the generous sponsor of your concert tonight ... Lady cats and gent cats, you may well be wondering who could be this wonderful, this well-connected, this perfect ... Well, there's nothing like perfect breeding to produce a perfect cat ... Allow me to introduce the beautiful ... the elegant ... the offspring of two grand champions ... the one and only *Nemesissy Lilac Masquerade!*'

CHAPTER FOUR

NEMESISSY

'Nemesissy?' Tagg repeated, looking at Sugarfoot for confirmation. 'Isn't that the name of one of the missing super cats?'

Sugarfoot's ears had pricked up too. 'It's got to be her. After all, how many Siamese cats called Nemesissy could there be?'

Everyone catcalled enthusiastically as the sleek lilac point Siamese female sashayed on to the stage, purring loudly. Her eyes were a deep purplish blue, her whiskers exquisitely styled and her face as perfectly triangular as that of her grand champion parents.

'Weren't the boys marvellous?' she called out in a strong husky purr of a voice. She paused to allow the cheers that followed to die down. 'My dearest feline citizens,' she continued, 'as many of you already know, I live with one of the cleverest human scientists in the country. Furthermore, I have what I'm sure you have all dreamed of having – utter control over that human.'

'Tell us your secret!' someone shouted.

Nemesissy smiled. 'It is ... well, let us say it's a power I was born with. I have only to look my human in the eye, tell him what I want and he rushes to do my bidding.'

Tagg gasped and looked at Sugarfoot. 'It's definitely her! Your mum said her power was hypnosis.'

'Must be,' Sugarfoot whispered back, searching for her mother's face in the crowd, eager to judge her reaction.

'I can feel your jealousy, fellow felines,' Nemesissy continued breezily, 'and believe me, if our situations were reversed, I would feel exactly the same. However, there is no need for envy, I can assure you. I wish to use *my* influence over my human pet to improve *your* lives. We are already building the most high-tech laboratories here. So, tell me, what worthy science projects would you like my human to undertake for you?'

'What about mouse-flavoured cat food? Can he invent us some of that?' a cat in the audience shouted as spluttery mews of mirth sounded around the room.

'Splendid idea! I will ensure he makes that

one of his top priorities,' Nemesissy replied.

The Siamese looked almost euphoric as she beckoned from the wings four young muscly cats who were carrying baskets of sardines in their mouths. 'My bodyguards will now distribute signed sardines to you all,' she told her delighted audience.

'My mum doesn't look that impressed. Nemesissy might not be missing, but where is my dad?' Sugarfoot hissed in Tagg's ear.

But Tagg was staring at his own mother, whose whiskers had shot forward and tail bushed up as she stared at one of the body-guards. He was a lean young tabby with grey paws, a white nose and a completely ginger tail. As the four bodyguards began throwing fish to the delighted audience, Melody kept staring at the tabby cat who was throwing his fish further back into the crowd than any of the others. In fact, he threw his last sardine with such force that it splattered against the back wall of the enormous room and exploded into tiny pieces.

At this point, Tagg's mother leaped up on to the stage.

Tagg heard her yowl loudly and the tabby turned towards her, suddenly looking a lot less confident as he miaowed in shock, 'MUM!'

Tagg watched Melody thoroughly lick the young tabby bodyguard as he squirmed under her rough tongue. So *this* was Rowdy, his super strong older brother?

In his excitement, Tagg totally forgot that he was meant to stay hidden. Without

thinking, he pushed his way to the very front through the departing crowd and jumped up onstage himself.

Rowdy immediately snapped into body-guard mode. Wriggling free of Melody, he unsheathed his claws and growled at Tagg.

'It's OK, Rowdy,' Melody miaowed quickly. 'This is Tagg, from my last litter. Your little brother.' She turned to face her younger kitten. 'What are you doing here? I told you to stay at home!' She gave him a growl that promised certain punishment later.

Rowdy's large paw had frozen in mid-air on its way to give Tagg's nose a warning blow. As he lowered it, he smoothed down his whiskers instead, grunting, 'Pesky kitten!'

'Hey, *I'm* a super cat too,' Tagg declared, puffing out his chest to show that he wasn't just any old kitten. 'Aren't I, Mum?'

Melody nodded and Rowdy gave her a disbelieving look, which made Tagg feel even crosser. Didn't he *look* super enough for Rowdy or something?

Rowdy wasn't the only one reacting to his declaration. Nemesissy had overheard them and now came closer to the trio, purring, 'Well, well, well … it seems we have a little family reunion – of three super cats no less!'

Suddenly, Glamour jumped on to the stage. 'Nemesissy, I'm so glad you're safe,' she gushed. 'There are super cats disappearing from Stoke Mewington. We thought you were one of them!'

'Super cats missing? Surely not!' the Siamese gasped, clutching a paw to her chest.

'Yes! The elastic couple – Bendy and Slinky. And my mate, Flash, disappeared two days ago! He was last seen on his way here to buy concert tickets.' She began to describe him.

Nemesissy was frowning. 'I'm afraid I haven't seen any of them. But I bet I know who's behind these disappearances!'

'Really? Who?'

She lowered her voice. 'Hamish the hit cat. His camp is somewhere in the woods behind this factory. That's why I hired so many body-guards. If I were you, that's the first place I'd look.'

Tagg had heard about Hamish and his crew. He knew they lived in a secret hideout in the woods and that every cat in the neighbourhood was afraid of them. Chester had pointed out Hamish to Tagg one day when they'd spotted him disappearing down a dark alley on the edge of town. The alley led into a rough wooded area where humans rarely went and no kittens were permitted to venture alone.

The gang members were known to be a ruthless and dangerous bunch – the kind of villainous group his parents had been sent to spy on and break up back in their crime-fighting days. Maybe they had a grudge against Flash and Bendy and Slinky from the old days?

Suddenly, they heard a big commotion from backstage.

They all went to see what was happening, and found the lead singer of One Purr yowling frantically at the other members of the band, who were all hissing at each other.

'What's the problem?' Rowdy asked.

'It's Thumper, our drummer!' the lead singer told them. 'He's disappeared!'

'What? How?'

'We were outside, about to hightail it out of

here, when Thumper said one of his drum-sticks was missing. He came back to look for it and now we can't find him.'

'He must be here somewhere,' said the band's guitarist. 'COME ON, THUMPER! I've got a bucketful of sardines waiting for me at home. Stop mucking around!'

Tagg whispered to Sugarfoot, 'This makes him the *fourth* super cat to go missing.'

The adult cats were looking extremely worried now.

'We should never have come to this dingy hole anyway,' the grumpy guitarist said rudely. 'I told you that message was fake.'

'What message?' Melody asked.

'Some big agent sent us a message saying she would come and see us if we did a concert here. If she liked us, she was going to get us our very own worldwide tour. I told the others I thought it sounded fishy – and not the good kind!'

Tagg turned to Nemesissy. 'But didn't you organise this concert?'

Nemesissy spluttered. 'Why, yes, of course I did. To announce my arrival in town. But I don't know anything about this agent! It's not my fault there are hit cats nearby.

In fact, Rowdy, take me upstairs to my quarters.' She shuddered. 'I just don't feel safe any more.'

'I guess hypnotising humans isn't that great a superpower if you get attacked by a hit cat,' Sugarfoot murmured as they watched Nemesissy sweep out, with Rowdy at her heels.

Glamour and Melody looked at each other in stunned silence, then quickly got down to business. They had to find Thumper, and any clue that might lead them to Flash and the other missing super cats.

Melody quickly steered the kittens down one plank of wood and up another to an open door that led into what must have been the dressing room for One Purr. On one side of the room were several plush cushions and

on the other a table with a mirror on top, in front of which lay several cat brushes and grooming combs.

'This time, I want you both to stay put like we asked you to!' she growled before dashing after Glamour and joining the search.

Just as it was starting to get dark the three bodyguards and the rest of One Purr came back to the dressing room to collect their instruments. They told them their mothers were still looking for clues.

'They've got to come back for us soon,' Sugarfoot said as she stood on her hind legs and peered out of the window.

'Let's go and find them,' Tagg suggested as his tummy grumbled loudly. 'I know they told us to wait but I'm starving!'

They left the dressing room and soon found an open door. In front of them was another stretch of dry wasteland, but here there were several outbuildings in various stages of disrepair. They couldn't see their mothers or any other sign of movement.

'You don't think they forgot we were here and went home without us, do you?' Tagg murmured nervously.

'Of course not,' Sugarfoot said, trying to sound more confident than she felt as she stepped out on to the exposed piece of land, breaking into a run as Tagg joined her.

They stopped abruptly as the grey wall of the first outbuilding loomed above them. There was no sign of Melody or Glamour as the two young cats gingerly approached the entrance, sniffing at the ground to check for their mothers' familiar scents.

Suddenly, they heard a high-pitched feline cry. It sounded like it came from the next building along.

His heart thumping, Tagg raced as fast as he could towards the sound, with Sugarfoot close at his heels. He turned a corner and there, collapsed on the dusty ground between the buildings, was Melody, blood gushing from a long gash on her side.

'Mum!' Tagg rushed to help her but froze when he realised how quickly the blood was flowing.

'N ... N ... N ...' she rasped, looking at him with glazed eyes before passing out.

Thankfully, Tagg and Sugarfoot weren't the only ones who had heard Melody scream.

Within seconds, Glamour was racing towards them.

'We didn't see what happened but she's bleeding really badly,' Tagg burst out in a shaky voice.

Glamour gave a startled mew as she took in the scene. Then she hunched down next to Melody, her belly almost touching the ground as she began to lick at the wound.

'It won't stop bleeding. The cut is too deep,' Tagg whispered, turning away to hide his face in Sugarfoot's side.

'It's OK – look,' Sugarfoot whispered softly in his ear. She butted his head gently to force him to look back at Melody.

Tagg looked and immediately saw that Glamour's lick was no ordinary one. The cat's pink tongue was now shining gold and sparkling, and as she licked the wound the blood flow slowed. After a few minutes Glamour stood back and Tagg saw that the bleeding had stopped and the wound had healed over.

'Mum's superpower is turning liquids to solids with her tongue,' Sugarfoot explained. 'She has a super lick!'

'It's a very *odd* superpower,' Glamour added, her tongue now small and pink again. 'But sometimes it's extremely useful. Come on. We have to get her to a vet. She's still very weak.'

They took Melody to the house of a human vet who was known for being both kind and good at her job, and as a consequence she frequently found injured cats on her doorstep. Tagg and Sugarfoot watched from across the road as she responded to Glamour's high-pitched mewing and opened her front door.

'Come on,' Sugarfoot whispered, sounding relieved. 'Let's go back to your place. Mum will stay with her.'

★ ★ ★

'Uncle Bill – WAKE UP!' Tagg called as he pushed in through the draughty cat flap, Sugarfoot behind him.

Wild Bill must have been in the middle of a very vivid dream because he leaped up with the energy of a cat half his age, yelling, 'Show yourself, you dirty varmint, or I'll snap you in two!'

'Wait! It's only me, Uncle Bill,' Tagg quickly reassured him.

'Cor blimey, I can't be jumping up like that at my age. What were you thinking, lad?'

'Sorry, but I have to tell you something ...' Tagg began. 'Another super cat went missing at the concert! Mum and Glamour were searching for him when Mum was attacked.'

Wild Bill was sitting right up now. 'Attacked? Who attacked her?'

'We don't know. She passed out so she couldn't tell us anything. We saved her and took her to the vet.' Tagg's voice cracked. 'Where's Dad? We need him to come back. Can we get a message to him?'

Wild Bill looked thoughtful. 'He'll be back soon, I expect, but until then you'll just have to tackle this without him.'

'Tackle this how?' Tagg asked. 'It's not like I'm super strong like Rowdy and Dad!' He'd thought about telling Rowdy what had happened and asking him for help but he was too scared to go back to the factory to find him. He also felt a bit uneasy that Rowdy worked for Nemesissy. There was something about the Siamese super cat that just didn't feel right to him.

'Super strength isn't everything, lad,'

Uncle Bill told him. 'And no super cat is invincible, just you remember that! It's why we have to combine our different powers and all work together.'

'Yes, but Sugarfoot and I don't have our superpowers yet,' Tagg pointed out, feeling frustrated. 'And since you've lost yours ...' He trailed off. He didn't want to hurt his great-uncle's feelings, but quite frankly he didn't think they made much of a team.

CHAPTER FIVE

HAMISH AND THE HIT CATS

The next morning Sugarfoot was following several paces behind Tagg as he led the way to the alley where he'd once seen Hamish.

'I can go on my own. You don't have to come,' Tagg told Sugarfoot, sensing that she was nervous.

'No, I'm coming with you,' she said with

determination. 'I just don't think it's your brightest idea, that's all. I mean, what if they catch us spying on them?'

'We won't let them! Don't worry, Sugarfoot, we'll be great at this! We both come from secret-agent families, remember! Spying on baddies is in our blood!'

Tagg suddenly remembered how, whenever he was spying on birds in the garden, they always seemed to sense his presence and fly away. Still ... he told himself firmly ... birds were stupid creatures that were very easily spooked.

They were approaching the alley when Sugarfoot noticed a sign pinned to a lamp-post above their heads. She jumped up on to a garden wall to take a closer look. 'Oh no!'

'What is it?' Tagg quickly joined her and

saw that it was a 'missing' poster for a black cat. The picture looked new and glossy, as if it had only just been put up.

Seeing the panic in Sugarfoot's eyes he attempted to reassure her. 'It probably isn't a super cat. Cats go missing all the time. It might have got lost or shut in somewhere.'

'I hope so,' Sugarfoot answered gloomily. 'Right. Let's get this over with.' She jumped off the wall and bounded along ahead of him until they reached the entrance to the alley. 'You're sure this is it?'

'Positive. Follow me.'

The alley led to a dead end, where a tall wooden fence barred their way. Tagg wasn't sure if he could jump that high. He tried to calculate exactly how tall it was and compare that with the highest leap he'd so far managed, which was from the floor on to the top of the mantelpiece at home. (The humans hadn't been too pleased when he'd skidded across the top, knocking off two china ornaments and a vase of flowers.)

I can do this, Tagg told himself sternly. He shuffled back a little, swung his hindquarters to prepare for the leap, and with fear fuelling his back legs and rushing through his whole body, he jumped. His hind legs scraped the top of the fence, but he cleared it and landed with a thud in a pile of muddy leaves.

Made it ... but Sugarfoot won't ... I'll have to do this alone, he thought.

'A bit of a noisy landing!' came a chirpy voice very close to his ear. 'Your stealth skills need some work if you're going to make it as a spy!'

'*What?*' Tagg was startled to see Sugarfoot sitting beside him, waiting patiently for him to recover.

'There's a hole in the bottom of the fence,' she explained with a cheeky grin.

Tagg scowled as he licked some moss from the fence off his fur. 'Then why didn't you tell me?'

'I only found it after you'd jumped. I think

it's a secret cat flap. Probably made by Hamish's gang. Come on – I'll show you. You might not feel like making that jump on the way back!' she teased.

But before either of them could move, they heard a noise of wood scraping as a large tortoiseshell cat pushed its way through the makeshift cat flap. Luckily, it didn't notice them sitting completely still in the leaves. The cat seemed intent on getting to wherever it was heading because it looked neither right nor left as it ploughed straight through the long grass.

'Let's follow it,' Tagg whispered. 'Maybe it will lead us to Hamish's den.'

They set off as quietly as they could, following at a safe distance behind the tortoiseshell cat on what turned out to be a trek through some overgrown gardens, until they reached a narrower alley, much muddier and weedier than the first.

After they'd trotted a short distance, Tagg spotted the first sign. It was an old plank of wood on which some sharp claws had carved out a message for other cats in bold scratch marks. It said:

HAMISH'S HITS THIS WAY!*

Following the sign they entered a narrow tunnel in a hedge, and it struck Tagg as strange that there was no evidence of any living creatures other than themselves and the cat they were following. A little way further along they spotted another

*translated from Cat Scratch for human readers

sign propped up against a tree trunk. This one read:

SPECIAL AUTUMN OFFER!
TAKE AN ENEMY OUT FOR HALF PRICE!

'What's that supposed to mean?' Tagg wondered aloud. 'Take them out *where*?'

Sugarfoot snorted in amusement. 'It's hit-cat slang! "Take an enemy out" means "kill them"!'

Tagg tried not to look shocked. 'I knew that,' he mumbled.

They passed two more signs scratched on to tree trunks. One read: **SECRECY GUARANTEED**, and the other: **DISPOSAL OF BODY EXTRA**. The prices were given in two types of currency – fresh mice or iced fish – and there were several package deals.

'Quick – someone's coming!' Sugarfoot hissed. She dived into the bushes, closely followed by Tagg.

Through a gap in the leaves he could see two adult cats walking towards them – a fat white one and the large tortoiseshell tom they'd been following.

'*Thirty* mice? How does he think I'm going to catch that many?' the tortie was grumbling in a very loud voice.

'You heard the boss. He doesn't care how.'

'Speak up. I told you my hearing's not what it used to be!'

'YOU HAD YOUR HALF-PRICE HIT AND NOW YOU HAVE TO PAY THE FULL AMOUNT! WE'RE NOT A CHARITY!' shouted the white cat.

'I'll give you charity! Hamish is greedy.

His quote is too expensive,' complained the tortie angrily.

'It's danger money!' replied the white cat. Seeing the tortie looking baffled, he repeated, '*DANGER* MONEY! We've bumped off SIX cats for you in the past year! It's like Hamish told you – it gets RISKIER each time we go back to the same place!'

'A simple poisoning is all I'm asking for this time. Or whatever else you like, so long as it happens while I'm sitting on my old girl's lap, so she doesn't suspect *me*.'

The white cat lowered his voice and leaned in very close to the deaf tortie's ear. 'Listen, why don't you wait and see if you feel differently about this new cat after a few weeks? It's not like you've given the last six much of a chance, is it? Maybe the old human only fusses over them so much because they're new.'

The tortie only grumbled as he left through the hole in the hedge.

Sugarfoot nudged Tagg with her wet nose and they exchanged a look.

As the white cat turned to go, Tagg stood on an especially crinkly leaf. Instantly, the cat's two white ears pricked up and its head turned towards their bush. Tagg's heart felt ready to leap out of his chest, and one look at Sugarfoot's bushed-up tail told him that she was also getting ready to bolt. But just at that moment there came more loud rustling from the hedge tunnel.

'Marshmallow, what's taking so long?' came a thick Scottish miaow as an enormous brown-spotted tomcat with orange eyes came

into view. This one looked like a cat who had been in a lot of fights. His ears were ragged and he had a scar down one side of his face.

'Hamish!' The white cat greeted his boss.

Tagg nearly fell out of the bush and Sugarfoot quickly choked back a mew of surprise.

'I was just getting rid of Daft Derek. Well, not "getting rid of" in *that* way, just—'

'Daft Derek deserves to be got rid of in *that* way,' Hamish interrupted, sounding irritated. 'Maybe then he'd finally stop complaining.'

Marshmallow snorted loudly. Then he said something that made Tagg's ears stand to attention. 'So, have you seen Nemesissy yet?'

Hamish gave a dismissive spit. 'Fruitcakes, her and her human! I saw them unloading more stuff last night ... no beds or cat baskets, just a load of laboratory equipment. Carried it all in by torchlight – well, the human did. The Siamese just sat there eating a kipper and watching him do all the work!'

'What sort of laboratory equipment?' Marshmallow asked curiously.

'Glass bottles and jars and some kind of glass incubator with tubes coming out of it. There were empty cages too – and one with a cover over it.'

'Do you think there were animals in that one?'

'Probably ... rodents, most likely. Hey, we'd better warn the gang not to eat any little furry bodies they find anywhere around here – who knows what poisons those lunatics have injected into them.'

Tagg was so distracted that he forgot where he was for a second. When he felt an itch on his neck, he automatically lifted his back leg to scratch it. The motion caused the bush to rustle.

'What was that?' Hamish hissed, and two seconds later he thrust his head into the bush where they were hiding.

Tagg and Sugarfoot yowled in fright as they found themselves face to face with the scariest, meanest-looking cat they had ever seen.

Run, Tagg tried to shout to Sugarfoot, but no words came out.

Hamish looked like a small panther as he brought his huge terrifying face even closer to theirs and gave a warning hiss.

'SPIES!' he growled. 'Get out here, you wee pests! Come out where I can see you!'

Tagg was rooted to the spot, too terrified to move. He felt Sugarfoot trembling against him.

'Don't make me come in there and drag you out!' roared Hamish.

'Allow me, boss,' said Marshmallow, nudging his way forward into the leafy bush and grabbing Tagg deftly by the scruff of his neck. Tagg yelped as he was dumped right under Hamish's nose.

His legs felt like jelly as Hamish glared at him fiercely. 'What are you doing here? Who put you up to this?'

'N-n-no one,' Tagg managed to stammer. 'We just … we just …'

'You're *just* trespassing on my land, you wee hooligan!' Hamish flexed his long claws with each word. They weren't super claws but they looked about as lethal as ordinary claws could get. 'You'd better tell me the truth – and quick!'

Tagg's mind was blank and his throat felt like it was paralysed.

'Don't worry, kids,' Marshmallow said cheerily, as he rudely dumped Sugarfoot beside Tagg. 'We hardly ever kill kittens. But if we do, we offer our super expensive "quick and painless" service. The boss is a big softie at heart!'

'W-we're looking for a cat called Flash,' Tagg blurted. 'He's gone missing. Someone told us that you might've ... might've ...'

'And what's it to you if we *have*?' Hamish hissed crossly.

'He's my dad!' Sugarfoot cried out indignantly. 'He's been missing for two days and ... and ...' She shuddered, unable to go on.

Marshmallow stared at her in surprise. 'We've had no work at all in the past fortnight, have we, boss?'

Hamish's voice took on a grumbly tone as he said, 'That's the way it is in this business. No work for weeks, then they all come at once, like ... like ...'

'Baby birds, boss?' his companion suggested.

'Exactly!' Hamish glared at them suddenly. 'But why did you come here? Who told you about us?'

'Nemesissy,' Sugarfoot blurted out.

'Nemesissy!' Hamish let out another dismissive spit. 'And you believed her? Just *how* do you two know her exactly?'

'My brother is one of her bodyguards,' Tagg answered.

'Really?' Hamish's eyes had narrowed. 'Well, tell your brother if he's got any sense he'll resign and find himself a more level-headed boss – like me! I wouldn't trust Nemesissy as far as I could throw her. NOW SCRAM!'

Tagg and Sugarfoot didn't need to be told twice. They took off as fast as they could, scrambling away through the undergrowth before Hamish could change his mind.

★ ★ ★

They finally stopped running, completely out of breath, when they reached the makeshift cat flap that led back to the alley. Just as they were about to go through it they heard big paws pounding the woodland floor behind them. They looked at each other in fright. What now?

It was Marshmallow. 'Don't panic. I'm not here to hurt you,' he miaowed as he saw their startled faces. Lowering his voice to a much fainter mew, he continued, 'Listen, there's something Hamish didn't tell you ... Nemesissy came to see him before she moved here. She wanted us to get rid of a cat colony that was already living in the factory ... but she said our price was too high and that she'd take care of it herself. And nobody's seen those cats

since. Just don't underestimate her, that's all. She's even more dangerous than Hamish.' He looked directly into Tagg's eyes as he added, 'You might want to warn Rowdy.'

And before either Tagg or Sugarfoot could respond, he disappeared back into the bushes.

'You never told him your brother was called Rowdy,' Sugarfoot murmured.

'What?'

'You just said your brother was Nemesissy's bodyguard. You didn't mention his name.' She paused. 'So how come Marshmallow knows it?'

CHAPTER SIX

TAGG THE SUPER CAT

Back at Tagg's house there was still no word from Chester. Wild Bill insisted there was no need to worry, but Tagg wasn't so sure. What if Chester had disappeared too?

Wild Bill demanded to hear everything about their adventure, and was particularly interested in the information they'd found out about Nemesissy.

'So her human's a scientist? Doing strange experiments on rats, you say?'

'That's what Hamish thinks. But do you think it's true, what Marshmallow said about Nemesissy?'

Wild Bill was looking thoughtful. 'Might be. There was a colony of strays living there before – not the sort to give up their territory without a fight. Then again … can you trust the word of a hit cat?' He turned and began to amble off towards his summer house. 'By the way,' he called back to them, 'Glamour came by while you were gone. Melody is on the mend, but she's to stay with the vet for another day or so. Glamour's gone to the factory to speak to Nemesissy. Melody told her it was a human who attacked her.'

'Nemesissy's human?' both kittens blurted out at once.

'We don't know. That's what Glamour's gone to find out.'

'We have to go after her,' Sugarfoot said. 'If the hit cats are right, then my mum could be in danger!'

'So could Rowdy,' Tagg added, realising he'd forgotten to tell Wild Bill about Marshmallow knowing Rowdy's name. But there was no time to mention that now.

As they took a shortcut across someone's garden, Tagg stopped suddenly, his nose twitching.

'What is it?' Sugarfoot whispered, freezing just behind him.

'A mouse,' Tagg hissed as he spotted

further movement under a nearby bush. 'I'm starving.' He squatted down into a low crouching position, but just as he started to wiggle his tail end ready to pounce, Sugarfoot let out a shocked screech.

Tagg jumped and the mouse scampered away in fright.

'What's wrong?' he demanded, scanning the area for danger and not seeing any.

'It's you!'

'What about me?'

'You've gone completely green!'

Tagg checked his paws and saw that they had turned the exact colour of the grass they were standing on. Shocked, he turned to check his tail. It was also green.

'You even *smell* of grass,' Sugarfoot said,

giving his fur a sniff. 'Oh … wow! This must be your superpower!'

'*Turning green?*' Tagg let out an indignant growl.

'Not just green! Keep thinking about chasing that mouse and go over to stand beside that house. Go on.'

Tagg did as she said. To his amazement, as soon as he stood against the painted grey wall his fur turned grey.

'Stick your paw in front of the back door,' Sugarfoot urged him. 'Just your paw! Go on!'

Tagg did so and watched as his paw turned exactly the same colour of blue as the door itself, as if it had been painted with the very same pot of paint. The rest of him stayed grey like the wall.

'Your superpower is camouflage!' Sugarfoot exclaimed. 'I can hardly see you or smell you. It's like you've totally blended into the background.'

'Camouflage?' Tagg was too shocked to say anything else.

'It's **AWESOME!**' Sugarfoot miaowed. 'You may as well be invisible! You'll be able to sneak around everywhere without being seen. It's the perfect superpower for a secret agent!'

'Really?' Tagg wasn't sure about 'awesome' – he'd been hoping for super strength – but he had to admit that his new superpower had lots of potential.

★ ★ ★

As they reached the hole Melody had made in the factory fence, Tagg started feeling nervous again. His superpower may have shown itself at last, but he didn't have a clue how to control it. Since he'd stopped chasing the mouse he was no longer disappearing into the background as they hurried along. Although when a car had roared past them, he'd turned green again, only this time it was the same shade of green as the hedge they were padding along beside.

'Your feelings must be triggering it,' Sugarfoot said. 'It switches on when you sense danger or when you need to chase something.'

'Yeah, well, it's all pretty weird if you ask me!' Tagg grunted.

'Don't worry. Even the weirdest

superpowers can come in really useful. Look at my mum! She saved Melody's life!'

'That's true,' Tagg said, and as he remembered that Glamour might be in danger, he quickly pulled himself together. 'Come on. We'd better hurry.'

They fell silent as they reached the factory. Tagg led Sugarfoot towards a metal spiral staircase at one end of the building. It seemed to be an old fire escape. 'This looks like it could be a way in,' he murmured. 'All we need is for one of those windows to be open ...'

'So what's the plan when we get inside?' Sugarfoot whispered as she followed him up the rusty steps.

Tagg didn't want to admit that he was making all of this up as he went along. 'Well, first we need to find your mum,'

he miaowed in a determined voice. 'Then ... well ...'

Sugarfoot suddenly felt an aggravating tickle in her throat and only just managed to stifle a cough. She wanted to continue up the fire escape behind Tagg, but the tickle in her throat wouldn't stop. Could it be a hairball? But she had coughed up hairballs before and none of them had felt like this. Her throat really hurt, as if hundreds of sharp fish bones had got stuck in it all at once.

'What's wrong? Are you OK?' Tagg asked in concern, waiting on the steps for her to catch up.

'I ... think so. My throat feels ... weird.'

'Your voice sounds hoarse. You'd better rest it.'

She gave herself a shake, remembering

why they were here. 'I'm OK. Let's go.'

Minutes later they were creeping along a gloomy corridor inside the building, heading for a door at the far end. The door had been left ajar and Tagg poked his head inside, only to be confronted with the strangest room he had ever seen. He was so taken aback that he let out a shocked little hiss.

He seemed to be in a science laboratory of some kind. In the centre of the room was a table with two glass incubators connected to each other by transparent plastic tubing. More tubing joined them to a strange-looking machine that had been constructed from various bits of metal joined together. The machine had all sorts of levers, wheels, cogs and other odd parts sticking out of it, plus

several thick cables attaching it to what Tagg
guessed were six enormous batteries.

'Over here!' mewed a weak voice, and he
turned to see a cage in the corner of the
room. The cage contained five cats, and Tagg
immediately recognised Glamour. She wore a
strange muzzle that stopped her from speaking properly – and from using her super lick.

Next to her a large male cat was sitting
on the floor, completely wrapped in thick

chains. Only his head had been left free. 'Mum! Dad!' As Sugarfoot raced past him into the room, Tagg realised the male cat must be her missing father, Flash. 'We have to free them, Tagg!'

There were three other cat prisoners in the cage, all secured by the same chains. Two thin black-and-white cats, who Tagg didn't recognise, were steadily devouring some old fish heads.

The last cat had a strange, glowing muzzle on the end of his tail and Tagg realised it was Thumper, the drummer from One Purr, whose superpower was to shoot firebolts from his tail. Only now he obviously couldn't.

Tagg knew they wouldn't be able to free any of them without help.

'You have to stop Nemesissy,' Flash grunted. 'She's using her superpower to control her human. He's invented that machine.' He pointed his nose at the strange contraption in the middle of the lab. 'I don't know what it does exactly but it can't be anything good. And we're going to be her test subjects.'

'How did they capture all of you?' Tagg couldn't quite believe that Nemesissy had managed to disable so many super cats.

'They shot us with a tranquilliser gun. When we came to, we'd been tied up and left here. Rowdy tried to stop them shooting Glamour today, so they shot him as well! The human tied him up with a super-strong rope he's invented. And Nemesissy is so angry she's going to feed him to her pet shark.'

Tagg felt sick. 'Oh no! Where did she take him?'

'The shark tank is in her private room on the top floor.'

'OK, I'm going up there. I'll come back as soon as I can and get you all out of here,' Tagg promised, trying to sound more confident than he actually felt.

Sugarfoot insisted on going with him.

Worried that he might be leading her

into more danger, Tagg lowered his voice and mewed, 'You do know I don't really have a plan, or any idea how to rescue Rowdy, don't you?'

Sugarfoot's whiskers twitched slightly as she whispered, 'Why else do you think I'm coming with you?'

At the very top of the staircase Tagg crossed a small landing and nudged open the door to Nemesissy's private quarters. With Sugarfoot close at his heels, he slipped silently inside.

He felt his heart beating furiously as he spotted Rowdy. His brother was bound and gagged and dangling helplessly in mid-air above an enormous glass fish tank. The tank contained a large shark.

Nemesissy suddenly whirled round to face them, making them both jump. 'Well, look who's here! The kitten rescue squad!'

She looked just as majestic as she had at the concert – her fur sleek and her lilac Siamese colouring as striking as ever. Her purple-blue eyes gleamed as she lifted up her perfectly pointed chin to regard them with undisguised contempt.

Tagg just gaped at her.

Nemesissy gave a mocking hiss. 'Come right in! I've been expecting you. How sweet of you to bid your naughty brother farewell.' She lifted a paw and lazily pointed it in the direction of her captive. 'How do you like my *super*-strong rope? Another of my human's amazing inventions! Do come closer and take a proper look!'

She was grinning as they nervously approached the tank. 'Don't worry about Sharky. I know he looks cross, but he'll be in a much better temper after he's eaten!' She snorted at her own joke. 'Sharks are so greedy they like to swallow their food whole,' she continued smoothly. 'I do hope he doesn't get indigestion.'

Meanwhile, Rowdy was struggling in vain against the glowing rope that bound him. It clearly contained some sort of weird energy that was even stronger than Rowdy's super-power – which was a very scary thought.

'You won't get away with this,' Sugarfoot said in a small but clear miaow.

Nemesissy laughed. 'Phooey! Why ever not? I've already got away with millions of evil deeds!'

'I don't understand,' Tagg interrupted. 'We're all super cats, just like you. Why would you turn against us? What is it you want?'

'What do I *want*?' Nemesissy sounded as if she found that the most stupid question imaginable. She was practically spitting as she continued, her eyes glinting crazily as her shrill miaows grew louder and louder. 'I want *your* superpowers as well as my own, of course! Why settle for one superpower when you can have them all? Can you imagine it, Tagg? Possessing all the superpowers in the world! Think how powerful I'll be!'

Tagg gulped. 'But how ... I mean, how can you ... ?'

'How?! My human is the cleverest and craziest scientist in the world – that's how! And using my superpower I have made him

invent a machine that extracts the super-powers from other cats and transfers them to ME!'

Tagg grunted as he realised she was talking about the machine in the laboratory.

'That *is* clever,' Sugarfoot began slowly, stalling for time. 'But there's one thing I don't understand – how do you expect your plan to work? I mean, we all know that when a super cat dies their superpower dies with them.'

'Quite right, my dear. Why do you think I'm having to keep all my captives alive instead of killing them straight away? Such a shame about Melody, by the way! I did so want those lovely super claws!'

'But why kill Rowdy?' Sugarfoot asked, trying to stay calm. 'Don't you want his super strength?'

'Rowdy?' Nemesissy gave an evil hiss. 'Rowdy's a different story. Rowdy betrayed me! *Me!* Luckily, super strength is a very common superpower. I can easily obtain it elsewhere. From Tagg's father, for example. Now – enough chatting. It's Sharky's dinner time … I just have to press this button here and a specially made knife will cut through the super strong rope. All designed by my very own human pet. You know, I don't rate humans on the whole, but occasionally you find one who's an absolute *gem.*'

CHAPTER SEVEN

GO SUPER CATS!

Everything happened at once.

Nemesissy slammed her paw down on the big plastic button and a deadly-looking knife on a metal arm shot out from the wall,

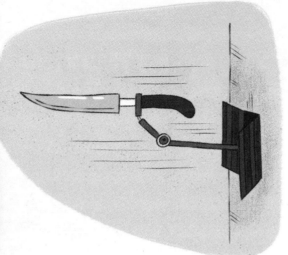

perfectly angled to cut the rope that was fastening Rowdy to the ceiling.

Sugarfoot started coughing again, only this time the tickle in her throat felt as if something much bigger than a hairball had got stuck. Her legs gave way beneath her as, from the back of her throat, came the most incredible yowl. It was a yowl she had no control over. She felt the floor vibrate under her and saw the look of surprise on Tagg's face. And that's when she realised what was

happening. This wasn't just any YOWL – it was a **SUPER YOWL!**

Everything in the room was vibrating now. A glass fell off a shelf and smashed on to the floor; blinds rattled; Nemesissy's fur ruffled and her ears flattened like a cat caught outside in high winds; mini waves formed on the surface of the water in the tank. The metal

arm protruding from the wall above them vibrated with the knife still attached, and instead of cutting the rope it merely nicked it.

Sugarfoot was too confused to take it all in. The phenomenal outpouring of energy from her throat had left her feeling shaky and exhausted.

Nemesissy glowered at her. 'A super yowl, eh? When you learn to control it that could be very useful! Now, if you've quite finished ... ?'

Sugarfoot knew she didn't have the energy

left to speak, let alone yowl again. Panicking, she scanned the room for Tagg. Where was he?

Clearly, Nemesissy was mystified by Tagg's disappearance too. Her tail grew bushier and bushier as she searched the room for him.

Luckily, Sugarfoot spotted him first. He was perfectly camouflaged and practically invisible, but she could just make out his movements as he climbed up a bookcase and leaped off it to land on his brother's super strong shoulders, grabbing the handle of the knife in his jaws and yanking it free.

But this movement caught Nemesissy's attention and she let out an angry hiss as Tagg cut the rope that bound Rowdy's legs and the rest of his body.

Nemesissy spat in fury as she saw the rope falling away from her prisoner. Now that Rowdy's legs were free, he began to swing them back and forth, his whole body moving like a pendulum as Tagg clung to his shoulders, the super strong knife held firmly in his jaws. Once they were swinging high enough,

Tagg waited
for exactly the
right moment
before cutting
through the
rope that
attached
them to
the ceiling.

Instead of
dropping straight
down, they flew
through the air in
an arc, landing with a
massive thud on the floor to one
side of the tank.

As he saw the hungry shark swimming
towards them, Tagg held his breath, only to

let out a sigh of relief as it banged its nose stupidly against the glass wall.

Meanwhile, Nemesissy was miaowing loudly for her human as she made a dash for the door. 'We have to free the others,' Tagg panted as Rowdy struggled to his feet. 'Can you help us?'

'Of course! I'll take over from here. You two just get yourselves out of here safely, OK?' Without waiting for a response, Rowdy bounded after Nemesissy.

Tagg and Sugarfoot stared after him.

'Like that's going to happen,' muttered Sugarfoot after a few moments.

'I know. We just saved his life and now he's treating us like babies! You wait – he'll probably need rescuing again in a minute!'

'We'd better go after him. Nemesissy's human is still around here somewhere.'

As they crept stealthily down the staircase, Sugarfoot whispered, 'Oh no … my throat's starting to tickle. I think I've got another super yowl building up.'

'Good,' Tagg whispered back. 'We might need it.'

'Yes, but I can't control it yet!'

They fell silent as they reached Nemesissy's laboratory. A human voice could be heard inside. 'You know it's very noble of you super cats to offer your services like this,' a man's voice was saying quite politely. 'Of course, there's even a tiny chance you could *survive* the superpower extraction ... though it's highly unlikely ... but even if you only live for a few minutes afterwards, you'll be lucky enough to see the masterpiece you've helped to create – a more powerful super cat than anyone has ever dreamed of. A feline of incredible power ... a feline who it will be every cat's honour to serve ...'

Loud, impatient miaowing interrupted this monologue. It was Nemesissy. 'Get the tranquilliser gun, you idiot! They'll be here in a moment!'

'Yes, ma'am. I'm presuming we're using the stun darts again, not the poisoned ones?'

'Yes. I want their superpowers. That little female has a most enchanting yowl. I could make great use of that!'

The ability to communicate properly with the human was a major part of Nemesissy's superpower, Tagg realised. It was a pretty awesome power – for a human to understand what you miaowed at them and then do your bidding without question. The possibilities were endless!

'I'm going to sneak in there and take a look,' Tagg whispered. 'I'm not sure where Rowdy is …'

He crept into the room, belly low on the floor as if he was stalking prey. The imprisoned super cats were still inside their cage and the rest of the laboratory seemed the same. There was no sign of his brother. Nemesissy and her human were standing beside the strange machine, loading darts into a weird gun that looked like a cross between a toy rifle and an extra-large water pistol.

Nemesissy suddenly let out a vicious hiss. 'HEY!'

Tagg jumped and just managed to stay quiet as he realised she wasn't yelling at him. Rowdy had come swaggering in through the door as if he owned the place.

'I went to have a little talk with the other bodyguards,' he told Nemesissy as he headed for the cage where the prisoners were being held. 'Gave them a demonstration of my superpower and told them to SCRAM!' He glanced out of the window and gave a satisfied purr. 'Good. I see they're following my advice.'

Nemesissy let out a nasty growl as she jumped down to confront him at floor level. 'You've got nerve, I'll give you that.'

Rowdy turned his back on her, using his super strength to bend the metal bars of the cage and create an opening big enough for the cats to escape through. But before he could release the imprisoned cats, Nemesissy rubbed her silky body against her human's ankle and ordered him to shoot.

As the human pointed the rifle, Tagg raced forward and leaped up to bite his arm, sinking his sharp teeth deep into the hairy flesh. The human was so shocked that he screamed and let go of the gun, which fell straight down on to Nemesissy's head, temporarily stunning her.

Then suddenly, from the open doorway, Sugarfoot let out an ear-piercing, high-pitched sound that grew and grew in volume, causing test tubes and glass jars and bottles of liquid to start rattling on their shelves. Even the big glass incubators were shaking.

'My experiments!' the human wailed, his attention diverted from Nemesissy, whose weak cries for help were blocked out by the racket Sugarfoot was making.

Meanwhile, inside the cage, Rowdy was using his super strength to release the captured cats. He made short work of the chains around Flash and the muzzle tied over Glamour's mouth, then he went to free Thumper, Bendy and Slinky. The whole time the room shook, as if in the throes of a diabolical earthquake.

'Please STOP IT!' the human was pleading hysterically as his precious glass bottles and jars full of long-nurtured experiments smashed and spilt their contents over the floor.

But Sugarfoot stayed rooted to the spot, mouth open and teeth bared, as her terrifying YOWL filled not just the entire room but the whole building.

'Tagg, take everyone out down the fire escape,' Rowdy yelled as cracks began to appear in the walls. 'Sugarfoot, tone it down a bit, will you?'

But Sugarfoot couldn't hear him.

'Uh-oh!' Tagg watched through the window as the rusty fire escape fell off the wall with a clatter.

'Don't worry. We can stretch our bodies out of the window and make slides down to the ground,' offered Bendy. Slinky nodded.

'Better still, I'll use my super speed to whizz us all away from here,' said Flash.

'Well, hurry. I think the building might be

about to cave in!' For the first time Rowdy sounded nervous – and that in turn scared Tagg, who tried to cross the room to Sugarfoot but found himself unable to get through the barrage of falling objects.

Glamour, Thumper, Bendy and Slinky were soon clear of the building. As Flash returned to collect the others, Rowdy used his superpower to bat away falling bricks and big lumps of ceiling as he crossed the collapsing laboratory to grab Sugarfoot.

Nemesissy and her human had taken shelter behind what was left of their precious extraction machine. The human must have finally heard Nemesissy's instructions above the din because suddenly he darted out from their hiding place and bent down to lift the gun from the floor.

Tagg spotted it, but by the time he'd yelled 'GUN!' Flash was already super-speeding him to safety, depositing him outside on the ground with the other super cats.

'Gun?' Flash queried in alarm, but just at that moment Sugarfoot's deafening super yowl stopped abruptly.

Tagg gave a hiss of fear and Flash didn't wait to ask any more questions before super-speeding off again in a cloud of dust.

Glamour came to stand with Tagg and the two of them held their breath as they spotted Rowdy out on the window ledge, his mouth holding a limp ball of black fur by the scruff.

'Is that Sugarfoot?' Tagg asked uncertainly.

'Yes. But why isn't she moving?'

Rowdy's front legs were stretched out and he was pushing against the window frame

with all his might. Tagg realised Rowdy was literally holding up the ceiling.

Flash was a blur of dark fur as he swept towards the pair on the window ledge, coming into focus briefly as he slowed enough to grab them. Then they were whizzing away again, through the falling debris, as the rest of the super cats stood willing them to make it.

Glamour and Tagg rushed to Sugarfoot's side as soon as Flash placed her and Rowdy gently beside them.

'She got hit,' Rowdy explained shakily. 'They were aiming for me, trying to stop us escaping … she threw herself in front of me … I *think* it was a tranquilliser dart.'

'Look!' gasped Bendy and Slinky as the whole building rumbled loudly. The next thing they knew there was a dark, uneven mass on the ground and thick grey dust filled the space where the building had just been.

'Bye-bye, crazy bad guys,' murmured Thumper.

'You're sure they didn't escape?' Bendy asked with a frown.

'Don't see how they could,' Slinky answered, coughing as he inhaled some dust.

'Ooh,' complained a small voice, and to

everyone's relief Sugarfoot was suddenly awake again, trying to escape her mother's icy lick.

'Thank goodness you're OK,' Tagg gasped, bending down and licking her too.

'I think we'd better leave,' Flash said as they heard sirens in the distance. 'The humans are on their way, and you know what a fuss they're bound to make.'

CHAPTER EIGHT

A PURR-FECTLY AWESOME ENDING

'Mum!' Tagg cried in relief when they got home to find Melody resting in her cat bed in the kitchen. Her middle was completely bandaged up, with shaved skin visible on each side. She looked tired and glassy-eyed. But at least she was safe.

'Are you all right, Mum?' Rowdy asked, coming through the cat flap behind Tagg.

'I'm still a bit woozy,' Melody replied. 'The vet gave me an injection for the pain.'

Since it was still the middle of the night their humans were upstairs in bed and the cats had taken over the kitchen. Wild Bill was over by the sink trying to open some food pouches, but he was having trouble using only his gums.

'Shall I do that?' Flash offered, his mouth watering at the prospect of food. 'Nemesissy hardly fed us and when she did it was always the same thing ...' He closed his eyes as if trying to block out the memory. 'If I never see a fish head for the rest of my life it'll be too soon.'

Thumper, Bendy and Slinky had gone home, but Sugarfoot's family had decided to stay at Tagg's house.

'We'll help too,' Glamour and Sugarfoot offered. Soon all three cats were ripping open the pouches for everyone to feast on.

'So where have you been?' Melody asked them curiously as Tagg snuggled up to her, taking care not to put any pressure on her injured side. 'Where did you find Flash?'

Mewing at top speed and constantly interrupting each other, Tagg and Sugarfoot explained everything. 'So, you see, our superpowers came in just in time!' Tagg finished off breathlessly.

'Thank goodness,' Melody miaowed with a gentle purr. 'Though missions don't rely solely on superpowers, you know. You two also used your heads and worked together.' She gave Tagg a fond lick as she added, 'I'm really proud of you.'

'Thanks,' Tagg said, feeling a bit embarrassed by the lick. 'And ... well ... Rowdy helped a bit too.'

'*After* we saved him from that shark,' Sugarfoot clarified cheekily.

'For which I will be forever grateful,' Rowdy assured her with a dramatic shudder.

'There's one thing I don't understand,' Tagg said in a puzzled voice. 'How come you were working for Nemesissy in the first place, Rowdy? Didn't you *know* she was evil?'

'Well, actually, I did. That was the whole point ...' He gave an apologetic mew. 'I couldn't tell you before but I've been working undercover. My mission was to spy on her.'

'*Mission?* You mean like a secret-agent mission?' Tagg felt an excited tingle run down his spine.

'Yes. I was recruited by Topaz Top Cat a few months ago ... but it's all been top secret until now.'

'Topaz *Top Cat*? Isn't that the cat Mum and Dad and Uncle Bill used to work for?'

'Yep! She's been putting together a new team of cat agents and—'

'Wait ... Topaz is back in action? Why didn't she contact me?' Wild Bill snorted crossly.

'Well ... you kind of need to be able to stay *awake* to rescue other cats and do all that spy stuff, Uncle Bill. And what with all your super teeth falling out ...' Rowdy said.

Wild Bill gave him a fiery glare. 'Cheeky youngster! I'll have you know my gums are still capable of giving *you* a good nip!' He broke some rather smelly wind, shooting a glare at Rowdy as he barged through the cat flap.

'What made Topaz suspect Nemesissy?' Melody asked curiously.

'She got a tip-off from one of her other agents, who's deep undercover in a gang of hit cats. She sent me to work for Nemesissy so I could gather more information.'

Remembering the big white hit cat who had warned them about Nemesissy, Tagg mewed, 'Is the undercover agent called Marshmallow?'

'You met him, didn't you? Nerves of steel, that one. If they found out who he was, they'd kill him in an instant. So you mustn't mention his name to anyone, OK?'

Suddenly, they heard a noise outside. They all turned to look as a big orange head pushed in through the cat flap.

'Dad!' Tagg mewed in delight, running to greet his father.

'Chester! You're home!'

'Melody? What happened?'

After Chester had been reassured about Melody's condition and had been reunited with Rowdy and the others, he announced proudly, 'We have an important visitor. She has just been waylaid by Uncle Bill,

who spotted us in the garden, but she'll be here any minute.'

'Who is it? Not *Topaz*?' Melody winced as she tried to sit up straighter. 'Chester, don't leave her out there with Uncle Bill, for goodness sake! Escort her in.'

But before he could, their cat flap opened and a most unusual cat made her entrance. She had short grey fur, a round face and the biggest greeny-blue eyes Tagg had ever seen. He guessed she was older than his parents, but not as old as Great-Uncle Bill.

'Topaz!' Melody greeted her in delight. 'How wonderful!'

'Topaz Top Cat!' Tagg blurted in awe.

'Good evening, ma'am,' said an unusually polite and serious Rowdy.

'Agent Rowdy!' their visitor exclaimed. 'What news of our target?'

'Eliminated, ma'am,' Rowdy replied solemnly.

'We're sure? We actually have a body?'

'The humans are there at the moment but—'

'A whole building's squashing her, so she's got to be as flat as a pancake by now,' put in Sugarfoot helpfully.

Topaz turned her gaze to the young cat. 'And you are … ?'

Rowdy quickly introduced Sugarfoot and Tagg. Topaz was clearly impressed when she heard how they had rescued Rowdy and helped thwart Nemesissy's evil plot.

'It sounds like we have two new recruits in the making,' she said with a surprisingly

Cheshire-cat-style grin. 'How would you kittens like to join my new team of agents? I have another mission that I think you two would be perfect for.'

Sugarfoot and Tagg both immediately leaped up, their tails bushy with excitement.

'Yes, please!' Sugarfoot mewed. 'That would be brilliant!'

'She means SUPER!' Tagg added, twitching his whiskers cheekily.

MEET THE

MELODY
Superpower: Super claws!
Extremely sharp claws that can
cut through anything
Status: Inactive

CHESTER
Superpower: Super strength!
So strong he can jump huge
distances
Status: Inactive

TAGG
Superpower: Camouflage! Ability to
disguise himself to his surroundings,
making himself almost invisible
Status: New recruit

GLAMOUR
Superpower: Super lick!
A sparkly gold tongue that can
turn liquids to solids
Status: Inactive

SUPER CATS!

FLASH

Superpower: Super speed!
The fastest cat the world
has ever known
Status: Inactive

SUGARFOOT

Superpower: Super yowl!
A yowl so deafening it can
shatter glass
Status: New recruit

ROWDY

Superpower: Super strength!
So strong he can hold up
crumbling buildings
Status: Active agent

WILD BILL

Superpower: Super teeth!
Incredibly sharp teeth that can
bite through anything
Codename: The Gnasher
Status: Retired. More suited to naps now

COULD YOUR PET BE
SUPER?

Take this quick quiz!

1. Does your pet mostly ...
a) Sleep?
b) Play?
c) Spend time outdoors?

2. What does your pet like doing most?
a) Sleeping
b) Trying out new things
c) Getting into mischief

3. Does your pet have lots of friends?
a) No, it's quite solitary
b) Maybe. Certainly lots of different animals visit our garden
c) Yes! So many I lose track

4. **Have you ever seen your pet do something incredible?**

a) Not really, they just sleep a lot

b) Once I thought they had completely disappeared, but when I looked again they were right there ...

c) Yes! My pet once ran out of the garden so fast it burst through the fence!

 Mostly a – Your pet might have had superpowers once, but they have probably retired now, like Uncle Bill

 Mostly b – Your pet could have superpowers ... keep watching to see if any develop

 Mostly c – Your pet definitely has superpowers! Wow!

LOOK OUT FOR MORE

**SUPER
CATS**

ADVENTURES!

COMING SOON!

GWYNETH REES

Gwyneth Rees is half Welsh and half English and grew up in Scotland. She studied medicine and qualified as a doctor before she became a full-time writer. She lives near London with her husband, two young daughters and one noisy cat.

BECKA MOOR

Becka Moor is a children's book illustrator and storyteller living in Manchester. You can find her illustrations in a variety of fiction books and series as well as picture books. She has an obsession with cats and loves anything a bit on the quirky side.